Discussion Questions for Kids and Parents

In the book, Radar explains that the animals in the shelter ended up there for lots of different reasons. Can you think of some reasons why a dog or cat would be in a shelter?

What do you think animals in shelters dream about the most?

What do animals need to be healthy and happy?

Why is it a good thing to adopt animals from a shelter?

Radar is excited to see puppies on the plane. Most people love puppies and kittens. How might this be a problem?

What are some ways YOU can help homeless animals?

RADAR'S DREAM

In my dream, I'm flying. Not super high—
I can still see the ground, but I'm free.

No cages.

No hard floor.

Just warm sun and the rush of fresh air on my face.

I have the dream all the time. But today it seemed so real, and at the end I floated down from the sky and ran right into the arms of a smiley kid who was calling my name! He hugged me and told me I was home.

But then I woke up.

Hi, I'm RADAR.
They call me that because of my big ears.
I like my big ears because I can hear everything.

I can hear people coming way before they get to my kennel.

I can hear them when they whisper.

And sometimes I can even hear birds singing outside, and I think about my flying dream.

I live here at the shelter with lots of other dogs—and cats, too.
They're nice to us here, and a couple of times a day they take
us out the back door to pee. We ended up in this shelter for
different reasons—not because we're bad—but because we
haven't found the right person to love us forever.

That's what we all want—a FOREVER home.

Most days are the same, but today was different—*really* different. One of the regular people came to my gate, but I could tell it wasn't just to take me out to pee. She was excited. So I got excited. To tell the truth, I almost peed right there!

She stopped and talked to another lady who put her hand out for me to sniff. (Flowery!)

Then the flowery-smelling lady scratched me behind my ears and led me right out the door— the FRONT door!

Next thing I knew I was riding in a car with the sun on my face and my big ears flapping in the wind. It reminded me of my flying dream!

I didn't know where we were going, but I was happy. The flowery lady seemed happy, too.

After awhile the car stopped by a big field. All I wanted to do was run. It had been so long since I had room to *really* run. And if you run fast enough, you can make your own wind!

Then my big ears heard a new sound getting closer—a man's deep, growly voice. I'm never sure about new people. I've known some who were not so nice. When this man reached us he held out his hand. He had bright, kind eyes and fur under his nose!

He stroked my neck and said, "Hello there, Radar." I don't know how he knew my name, but I liked the way he said it.

The flowery-smelling lady handed the growly-voiced man some papers, and we all walked over the warm ground toward...

...THE STRANGEST LOOKING CAR I EVER SAW. It looked like a big, shiny bird with a pointy beak and two big whiskers!

The growly-voiced man started talking, but I didn't know what he was saying. Was he wanting me to get in that crazy bird-car? He said my name in a nice way—but I still didn't move.

Then I heard a different voice—and
finally words I DID understand.
"Tally Ho, Radar!
'Tis a beautiful day to fly!"

A little dog stood on the wing of the crazy bird-car.

"My name's McCloud, but everyone calls me 'Mac.' C'mon, then, Sonny. Nothing to worry about here. In fact, I'd say your worries are behind ye now. Hop aboard the Second Chance Express!"

Mac told me that the man was his two-legged dad. He's also the pilot of the crazy bird-car which he called an airplane. Mac is his copilot! They load the plane with homeless animals—just like me—and fly them to new places where they can have a real home with people who will love them forever—a FOREVER home.

I could hardly believe it.

"'Tis true," said Mac. "There are lots of other good people who save all sorts of animals—cats, rabbits, chickens, even snakes...If there's a better life waiting for an animal somewhere, we take 'em there."

"And today you're taking me somewhere?" I said.

"Aye," Mac said, "Today is your lucky day...it's everyone's lucky day!"

When we jumped into the plane I saw what he meant by "EVERYONE."
It was already full of dogs, big and small!

"Are we all going to the same home?" I asked Mac.

"Nay," he said. "Chance is on his way to Iowa, Ernie's going to Ohio,
and the pups are going all the way to Minnesota."

I wondered where all those places were, but there was no time to ask. The man shut the door, gave Mac a "thumbs-up" and started the engine. The three of us big dogs in the back looked at each other, too excited to talk. The puppies were too excited to be quiet.

I felt the wheels of the airplane start rolling faster and faster, until suddenly I couldn't feel them at all. I looked out the window and saw the ground moving away and the flowery lady getting smaller and smaller.

WE WERE FLYING!

I'd never seen the tops of trees before. Ponds looked as small as puddles and cars looked like chew-toys.

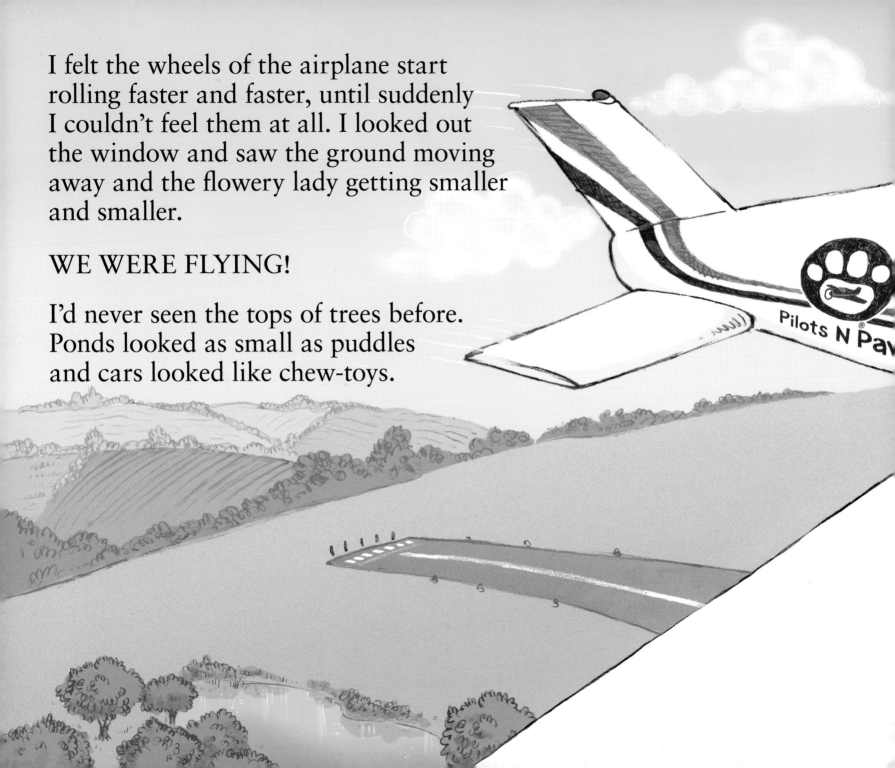

AMAZING!

BEAUTIFUL!

FLYING!

After all the excitement of the day
I started to feel a little sleepy.
The hum of the airplane's engine
was like a lullaby rocking me to sleep.

I guess it was the same
for the others.

In my dream I was flying—up with the birds, with the wind in my face. No cages. No cold, hard floor. It was the same dream I've had so many times before.

Only this time it was different.

This time, when I woke up, *everything* was different.

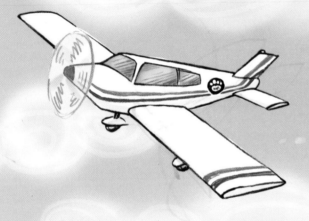

Published by WWW PILOTSNPAWS ORG, INC,
Landrum, S.C.
www.pilotsnpaws.org
ISBN: 978-0-615-88430-1

Patrick Regan is the author of more than 100 books for kids and adults.
He lives in flyover country with his family and their rescue dog, *Pearl*.
Learn more about Patrick at patrickreganbooks.com

Renée Andriani has illustrated numerous books and greeting cards.
She lives in Kansas with her family and Rosie & Boo, their two rescue pups.
You can see more of her work at randriani.carbonmade.com

ATTENTION: SCHOOLS
This book is available at quantity discounts with bulk purchase for educational use.
For information, please e-mail info@pilotsnpaws.org